Three Royal Birthdays!

By Andrea Posner-Sanchez
Illustrated by Francesco Legramandi & Gabriella Matta

A Random House PICTUREBACK® Book
Random House 🏠 New York

randomhousekids.com
ISBN 978-0-7364-3403-4
MANUFACTURED IN CHINA
10 9 8 7 6 5 4 3 2

Rapunzel's Big Day!

Although Rapunzel lives in a tall tower far away from friends and family, she still looks forward to her birthday every year. She even throws herself a party!

Rapunzel paints birthday decorations on the tower walls.

Rapunzel bakes herself a yummy cake. Pascal likes to help with the frosting!

"You can lick your tail when you're done," Rapunzel tells her chameleon friend.

Rapunzel plays party games and sings herself a happy birthday song.

But Rapunzel's favorite part of her birthday celebration happens after the sun goes down. That's when she gets to see all the lights floating by in the night sky.

"My birthday wish is to leave the tower and see the floating lights up close one day," Rapunzel says out loud. Do you think her wish will come true?

Tiana's Super Surprise

Tiana likes to keep busy working in her restaurant. So Charlotte has to do a bit of convincing to get her to take a day off.

"It's your birthday! The restaurant can close for one day," Charlotte tells Tiana as she pours her a cup of tea. "And I want to spend time with my best friend."

With Tiana occupied, Naveen springs into action. He is planning a surprise party back at the restaurant!

Tiana's mother puts the finishing touches on the birthday cake.

Naveen wraps a present.

"I think I left my ring on the table during dinner last night,"
Charlotte shouts as she and Tiana head into the restaurant.
"Help me look for it." That's the signal for everyone to get ready
for the birthday girl!

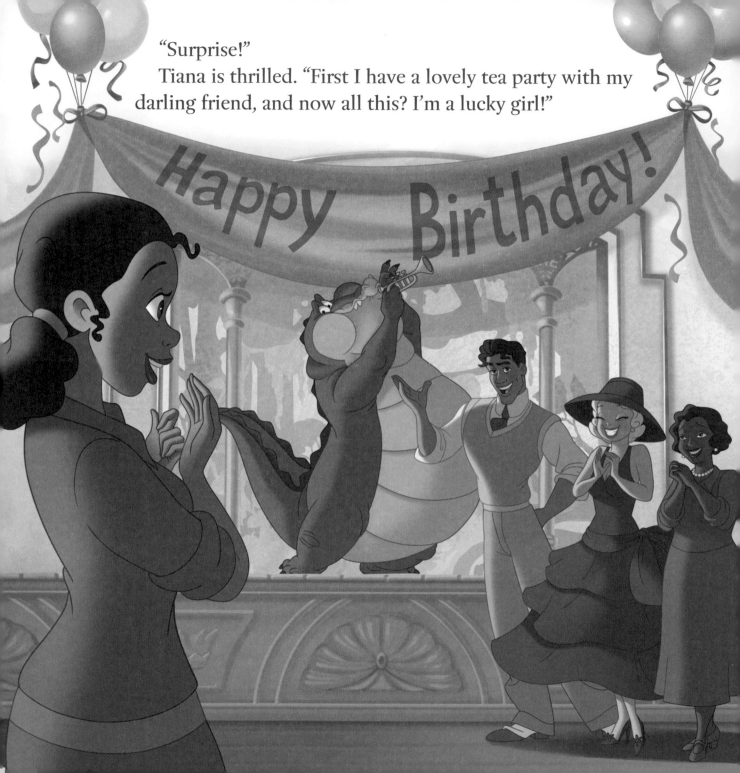

"Surprise!"

Tiana is thrilled. "First I have a lovely tea party with my darling friend, and now all this? I'm a lucky girl!"

Happy Birthday!

"Happy birthday," Naveen says as he hands his gift to Tiana. She opens the box to find a locket with a picture of her father inside.

"I'll treasure this always!" she says, hugging Naveen. "Thank you for the wonderful birthday surprises!"

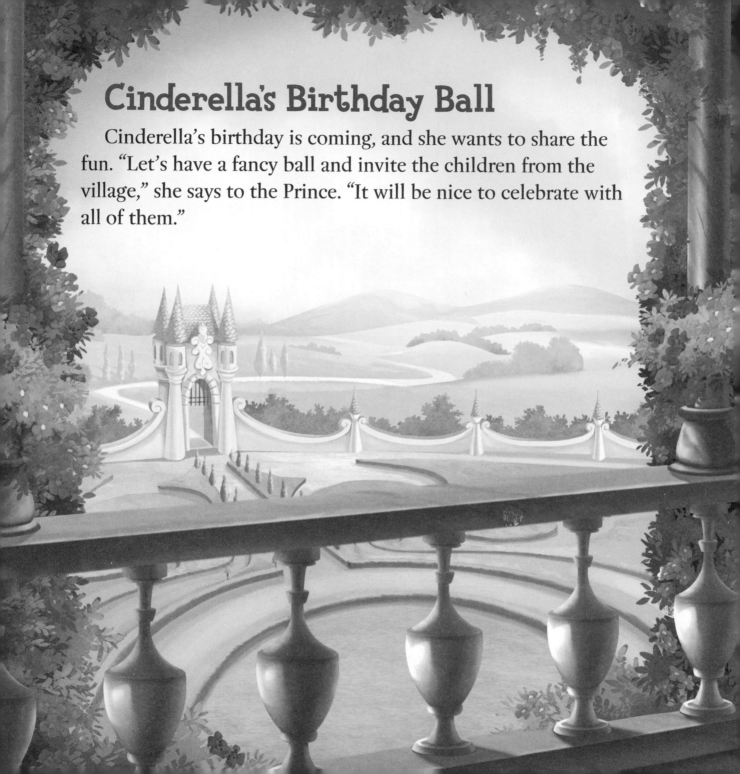

Cinderella's Birthday Ball

Cinderella's birthday is coming, and she wants to share the fun. "Let's have a fancy ball and invite the children from the village," she says to the Prince. "It will be nice to celebrate with all of them."

The Fairy Godmother sends out magical flying invitations.

Cinderella helps the royal chef bake cookies and cupcakes.

It's time for the birthday ball! Cinderella welcomes the children into the castle.

After a lot of good food and dancing, Cinderella makes an announcement.

"Thank you for sharing my birthday with me. Now I have a special treat for all of you!"

The Fairy Godmother waves her wand, and a wrapped box floats down to each child.

A little girl walks up to the princess and says sadly,
"But we don't have a birthday gift for you."
"Seeing all of your smiles is the best present I could
ever receive!" Cinderella tells her.

Princess Party Fun

You can throw your own princess birthday party! In addition to the Pin the Tiara on the Princess game included in this book, here are more ideas for games and activities you can do with your guests:

Let Down Your Hair

Before your guests arrive, cut some pieces of yellow yarn, each about 3 feet long. Tie or tape little treats, such as sticker sheets, plastic toys, and lollipops, to the end of each piece. Put all the yarn in a big bag and leave the ends without the treats hanging out. During the party, allow each guest to pull one strand of Rapunzel's hair to get a surprise!

Kiss the Frog

Get some red poster board and ask an adult to help you cut out shapes that look like lips. Make enough so everyone at the party can have one. Draw a picture of a frog on a piece of paper and place it on the floor. Have your guests stand about a foot away from the frog. Then take turns trying to toss the lips onto the frog to give him a kiss.

The Lost Slipper

Have one guest hide a glass slipper (or any type of shoe). Then you and your friends try to find it. As you get close to the hiding place, the hider can say you are getting warm. If you move away from the hiding spot, he or she can say you are getting cold. When you're hot, that means you've found Cinderella's lost slipper! Then it's your turn to be the hider.

Dress-Up Relay Race

You will need some dress-up clothes for this game. Divide your friends into two teams. Have a pair of shoes, a gown, a pair of gloves, and a tiara ready for each team. When an adult calls out, "Bibbidi bobbidi boo!" the first player on each team puts on everything in their pile of dress-up clothes. Then they run to a marked spot and back. They quickly take off the dress-up clothes, and the next person in line does the same thing. The first team to have all its players finish getting in and out of the clothes wins!